Pebble® Plus

BIRDS OF PREY

Golden Eagles

by Melissa Hill

Consulting Editor: Gail Saunders-Smith, PhD

Consultant: Jessica Ehrgott, Bird and Mammal Trainer, Downtown Aquarium, Denver

CAPSTONE PRESS
a capstone imprint

Pebble Plus is published by Capstone Press,
1710 Roe Crest Drive, North Mankato, Minnesota 56003
www.capstonepub.com

Library of Congress Cataloging-in-Publication Data
Hill, Melissa, 1975–
Golden Eagles / by Melissa Hill.
pages cm.—(Pebble Plus. Birds of Prey)
Includes bibliographical references and index.
Summary: "Describes the characteristics, habitat, behavior, life cycle, and threats to golden eagles"—Provided by publisher.
Audience: Ages 5 to 8.
Audience: Grades K to 3.
ISBN 978-1-4914-2090-4 (library binding)
ISBN 978-1-4914-2308-0 (paperback)
ISBN 978-1-4914-2331-8 (eBook PDF)
1. Golden eagle—Juvenile literature. I. Title.
QL696.F32H55 2014
598.9′423—dc23 2014032768

Editorial Credits
Jeni Wittrock, editor; Peggie Carley and Janet Kusmierski, designers; Svetlana Zhurkin, media researcher; Katy LaVigne, production specialist

Photo Credits
Getty Images: Ben Cranke, 13; Newscom: Design Pics/John Hyde, 5, Photoshot/NHPA/Jordi Bas Casas, 17, Photoshot/NHPA/Laurie Campbell, 19, Photoshot/NHPA/Mark Hamblin, 9, VWpics/Gerard Lacz Images, 21; Shutterstock: balounm, back cover (background), craigbirdphotos, 11, Erni, 7, Giedriius, 15, James K. Troxell, 1, Kenny Tong, cover, back cover

Note to Parents and Teachers

The Birds of Prey set supports national science standards related to life science. This book describes and illustrates golden eagles. The images support early readers in understanding the text. The repetition of words and phrases helps early readers learn new words. This book also introduces early readers to subject-specific vocabulary words, which are defined in the Glossary section. Early readers may need assistance to read some words and to use the Table of Contents, Glossary, Read More, Internet Sites, Critical Thinking with the Common Core, and Index sections of the book.

Printed in the United States of America.
010926R

Table of Contents

Home on the Range

A big brown bird waits on a cliff. She watches the ground below. She's a golden eagle hunting for her next meal.

Golden eagles live near grasslands, plateaus, and mountains. They are found in North America, Europe, Asia, and Africa.

Perfect Predator

Golden eagles are one of the largest raptors. They weigh up to 13 pounds (6 kilograms). Their wings spread out 7.5 feet (2.3 meters).

These birds see very well. Golden eagles can spot their prey from up to 2 miles (3 kilometers) away.

Golden eagles are fast flyers. They dive through the air over 100 miles (161 km) per hour. To grab prey eagles use their big feet.

On the Menu

Golden eagles hunt mainly rabbits. Foxes, snakes, and birds are on eagles' menu too. If there's no other food, eagles will eat dead animals.

Eagles hold prey with their strong feet and curved talons. Their sharp, hooked beaks are perfect for ripping and eating meat.

Golden Life

Golden eagles keep the same mate for life. Each year the pair raises one or two chicks. Golden eagles live up to 30 years.

Dangerous Times

In some places golden eagles are endangered. Laws in North America help keep eagles and their homes safe.

Glossary

chick—a young bird

endangered—in danger of dying out

mate—one of a pair of animals

plateau—an area of land that is flat but rises higher above the land around it

predator—an animal that hunts other animals for food

prey—an animal that is hunted by another animal

raptor—a bird that hunts using its feet

talon—a sharp, curved claw

Read More

Bodden, Valerie. *Eagle.* Grow With Me. Mankato, Minn.: Creative Education, 2014.

Guillain, Charlotte. *Soaring Eagles.* Walk on the Wild Side. Chicago: Raintree, 2013.

Hill, Melissa. *Red-Tailed Hawks.* Birds of Prey. North Mankato, Minn.: Capstone Press, 2015.

Internet Sites

FactHound offers a safe, fun way to find Internet sites related to this book. All of the sites on FactHound have been researched by our staff.

Here's all you do:

Visit *www.facthound.com*

Type in this code: 9781491420904

Critical Thinking Using the Common Core

How do golden eagles hunt and catch their prey?
(Key Ideas and Details)

What animal is the main prey of golden eagles? What else do they eat?
(Key Ideas and Details)

Index

Word Count: 195
Grade: 1
Early-Intervention Level: 14